Flour Sack Flora

Deborah L. Delaronde

❧ Book Design by: Sherry M. McPherson ❧

Pemmican Publications Inc. gratefully acknowledges the assistance accorded to its publishing program by the Manitoba Arts Council, Canada Arts Council and the Book Publishing Industry Development Program.

National Library of Canada Cataloguing in Publication Data

Delaronde, Deborah L., 1958-
Flour sack friends / Deborah L. Delaronde.

(Flour sack series)
Includes bibliographical references.
ISBN 1-894717-18-X

I. Title. II. Series: Delaronde, Deborah L., 1958- . Flour sack series.
PS8557.E4254F462 2003   jC813'.54   C2003-911238-1

Town seemed far away as they traveled over miles and miles of gravel road scouting for birds or animals through clouds of dust. Flora had always wanted to see what a town looked like and was curious about the people who lived there. But there was one thing that Flora wanted to see more than anything in the whole world.

"Isn't this wonderful Mucky?" she said to her pet frog. "We're reaalllly going to town!""Let's hope the store sells dolls," she said. "Once we see how they're dressed, I can ask grandma to sew one for me."

"Grandma can sew all kinds of things, let's hope she can sew a doll, too."

Dad parked the car in front of a building with a sign "Village General Store."

"We're here, Flora!" Mom said looking back. "Please don't touch anything in the store," she warned. "If you should break something, we would have to pay for it."

"I won't," Flora promised. "I'm just shopping for dolls to see how they're made and maybe buy some candy."

Dad set a bag of seneca roots on the counter to pay for their supplies and passed a handful of shopping lists to the storekeeper, Mr. Murdock.

When Flora's mom and dad left to do their shopping, she went exploring for dolls.

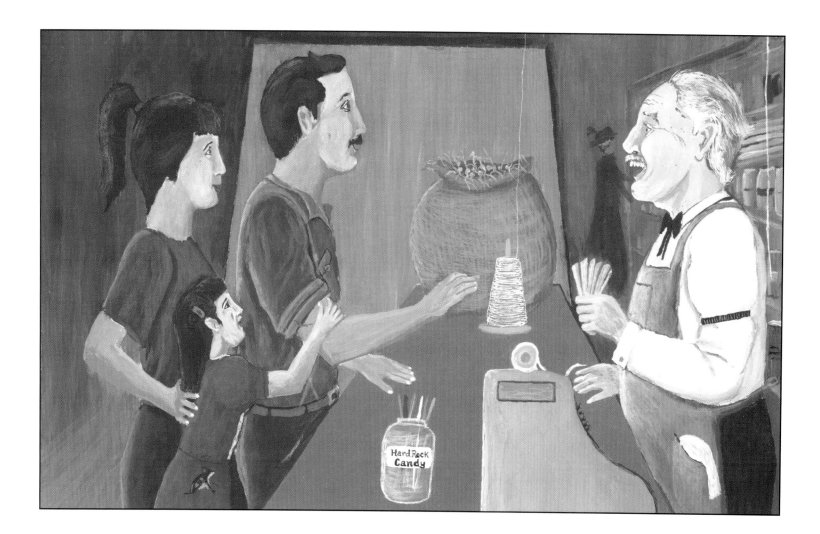

Flora walked between two rows of shelves packed with food and supplies. Then, there they were......*beautifully dressed dolls*.

But as Flora walked towards them, an elderly lady's beginning smile turned to horror.

Her eyes widened, her mouth fell open, she screamed and turned to run.....

......but tripped and stumbled pulling down a spool of lace and a jar of buttons.

As the lady straightened her dress, she said sternly to Flora, "Young lady, don't you know you shouldn't bring a FROG into a store?"

"We're very sorry," Flora mumbled.

Flora's mom whispered gently, "I think it would be better if you and Mucky were to sit outside and wait."

Flora's lips trembled in disappointment. How could she ask grandma to sew a doll for her when she didn't get to see what they looked like?

The girl from the store brought a bowl of water and placed it beside Flora.

"I'm Myrtle," she said. "Your mom said you had your heart set on looking at the dolls in our store. So......I brought one of mine for you to see."

"Is this your first time to town?" she asked as Flora closely inspected the doll.

Flora nodded shyly and said, "I always wanted to see what a town looked like. But I also wanted to see the dolls in the store so I could ask my grandma to sew one for me, too."

"Well.....since you can't see the dolls, maybe I can take you on a little tour of the town," Myrtle said.

Myrtle first led Flora to the docks.

"So...what do people do here?" Flora asked.

"The fishermen come in around noon and sell their fish to the packing house," Myrtle said. "People can then buy fish with money or trade with things like food, tools or help unload boxes of fish."

She then led Flora to the park.

"On really nice days, farmers set up tables to sell their fruits, vegetables, used clothing and crafts,"she said.

Myrtle and Flora went to look at the growing display of items.

A bright flash of color drew Flora's eye to a flower patterned dress. Then looking at Myrtle's doll, she had an idea.

"This would look great as a doll's dress," she said thoughtfully.

Seeing that Flora was a child the lady said, "I can sell you that dress for 30 cents."

Flora then remembered what Myrtle had said about work and trading.

"Umm....I can pay 25 cents," she said. "But, I'm wondering if you have any work for me to do so I can buy this dress?"

"Wellll....," the farm lady said thoughtfully.

"You can fold the clothes in neat piles."

"And....unload baskets of fruits and vegetables. That would be enough to pay for your dress," she said.

Flora and Myrtle returned in time to help load and pack the car carefully so that everything would fit.

"I'd like you to have some fabric that my mom used to sew my doll. Maybe your grandma can use it in sewing yours," Myrtle said.

"Thank you!" Flora said surprised.

"It was seeing your doll that gave me the idea to buy the dress," Flora said and gave Myrtle a hug.

They hadn't traveled far when they stopped to buy milk and cream. Dad placed a box of blueberries on the cupboard to trade for the rancher's dairy goods.

Mrs. Smith smiled, delighted at the blueberries and invited them in for lunch.

"Our daughter Flora and her frog Mucky had quite an experience at the store with Mrs. Flintock," he said as they sat down to a cup of tea and biscuits. Flora tried not to look disappointed as he explained what happened. He also spoke of Flora's interest in dolls.

"Would it be helpful to see one of the dolls that I sew? They are very much like the one I had when I was a child," she said to Flora, placing the doll on the table.

"Oh, yes!" Flora said excitedly but then became quiet when she saw the many layers of lace.

Flora then remembered what Myrtle had said about work and trading.

"Ummm.....if you have any of this beautiful lace left, I would gladly work for it," she asked hopefully.

"Well....," Mrs. Smith said thoughtfully.

"You can rip the seams out of these flour sacks," she said handing Flora a stitch-ripper.

"And iron these cloths for me. That would be enough to pay for your lace," she said and went back to visiting.

When Flora's jobs were done and they were on their way home again, Flora's mom and dad decided to stop and visit family.

The table was quickly set to feed the visitors a meal. While they ate, everyone talked and shared stories and news about family and friends. Flora felt more relaxed amongst her family and cousins until....

Flora's dad began the story of her first experience at the store with Mucky and Mrs. Flintock.

He went on proudly to describe how Flora had traded by working for the things she would need to dress a doll.

Laughing, cousin Margaret left but returned with a beautiful doll with black hair wearing a fringed dress with colored beads.

"A good story always deserves a gift," she said and handed Flora the doll's moccasins.

"Thank you, cousin Margaret," Flora said.

"I think I now have everything I need to dress a doll," she said. "I can hardly wait to get home so I can ask grandma to sew one for me."

It was dusk when they arrived home and Flora was exhausted. Grandma had kept the fire going and had shared tea, bannock and jam with the neighbors who had waited for their supplies. She helped Flora and her parents with their groceries while everyone else was busy finding their own.

Grandma waited patiently while Flora and her dad took turns telling the story of her first trip to town. Flora then placed the dress, the plaid fabric, the lace, and the moccasins on the table as she explained how she was given some and how she worked for others.

"I never did get to see the store dolls," she explained. "I went to town hoping to see how they were made so I could ask you to sew one for me."

"But I did get to see some beautiful hand sewn dolls," Flora said.

She then sleepily described what her doll would look like and how she would use each piece to dress her.

Flora was so tired that she went to her room forgetting all about dolls.

Mucky lay sleepily on the pillow watching her.

"Even though I had a lot of extra work to do, I'm glad you came to town," she said giving him a goodnight kiss.

"The next time we go anywhere, though, you'll have to stay hidden in my pocket......," she mumbled as she fell asleep.

Flora woke the next morning to find grandma sitting on her bed.

Laying beside her was a doll wearing everything she had brought from town.

"I sewed the doll's body from left over flour sack fabric," grandma explained.

Flora was astonished!

"Thank you, Grandma. She's the most beautiful doll of ALL dolls!" she said giving both grandma and the doll a hug.

"I never thought that a doll of my very own could come from a little frog, a little work and a little help from family and friends."